P9-CLJ-245
BEES!?!
by RAY FRIESEN

PIRATE PENGUIN
VERSUS
NINJA CHICKEN
by RAY FRIESEN

Other books by Ray Friesen

PPvsNC: Troublems with Frenemies
PPvsNC: Escape from Skull-Fragment Island

Lookit! A Cheese Related Mishap
Lookit! YARG!
Lookit! Piranha Pancakes
Another Dirt Sandwich
Flamboozled!
Cupcakes of Doom

ThunderLizard Ranch
  Book 1: Raptor Trapdoor
  Book 2: Qwakasaur Roundup
  Book 3: T-Rex Puppies

(as J. B. Hivemind)
  The Princess and the Pterodactyls
    (with Joe Heath and Vincent E.L.)
  Road Trippy
    (with Joe Heath and Chris Cherry)

Small Gods: A Discworld Graphic Novel
Written by Sir Terry Pratchett
Adapted by Ray Friesen

Marmaduke Mousington
Based on the works of Josh Kirby
Adapted by Ray Friesen

A to Z asaurus
Written by Ray Friesen
Illustrated by Michael Spiers

Fairy Tales I Just Made Up!
Written by Ray Friesen
Illustrated by A Bunch of Other People

Cats Committing Crimes
Illustrated by Ray Friesen
Written by A Bunch of Other People

www.RayFriesen.com

Editor in Chief: Chris Staros

Published by Top Shelf Productions, an imprint of IDW Publishing, a division of Idea and Design Works, LLC. Offices: Top Shelf Productions, c/o Idea & Design Works, LLC, 2765 Truxtun Road, San Diego, CA 92106.

Visit our online catalog at www.topshelfcomix.com.

ISBN 978-1-60309-497-9

Printed in China

25 24 23 22 21   1 2 3 4 5

AND NOW!

THE TOP SECRET (MADE UP) ORIGIN STORY OF YOUR PAL (AND MINE):

PIRATE PENGUIN

Once upon a long time ago, the Ice Planet Shoutball was invaded by Volcano Monsters from Beyond Space!

The Super Braintelligent Space Penguins who lived on Shoutball were allergic to lava, so they sent their second to last hope, ME, in little baby-egg form rocketing towards the Planet Neptune!

(Their aim was bad, and I crashed into Earth instead).

I landed in the underwater city of Hamlantis, and was raised by a fierce tribe of tiger shark warriors.

They named me Piratio Von Pengarrr, which in their language means "Beautiful Cool Dude."

I grew up, mostly, and took up freelance boat-robbing to pay for college.

Then, came the day of my terrible motorcyle accident...

Waugh!

TRIP!

Sinister government employees from the Fire Library captured me, and rebuilt my bones using highly advanced robot bone technology from the distant past. Free of charge!

I busted out of their secret laboratory in the back of the old abandoned Post Office on the very day they released me from their mind-controlled assassin training program for chewing too loudly.

I bummed around The Galapagos for a few months, during which time I defeated a Vampire Dragon at tennis, for which she granted me a magic wish.

RAWR! Good game, nerd!

Apparently my deepest heart's desire was for a best pal/nemeisis that I could practice my kicking skills on forever.

And so a bunch of stink bugs wrapped around a piece of rotting pizza, and they transformed into that dreaded, stink monster The Nunja Chunkin.

Plus, I got FREE Moonicorn Princess™ Lollipop Smoothies for life from a completely different magic wish! And I all lived happily ever after.

THE END.

BUT ALSO, TO BE CONTINUED!

And then Ninja Chicken wrote their own book that completely contradicted Pirate Penguin's book, and they all lived snappily ever after.

PREVENGE
A Pirate Penguin Vs Ninja Chicken Cartoon Adventure
Hey Pirate Penguin-- want some pizza?
HECK YES! That would totally make my day!
All I've had to eat is that stuff I found under the couch.
PIZZA WITH PIZAZZ©
Great! Go do the dishes and maybe I'll give you a slice!
-BLINK BLINK-
WHY ARE YOU SUCH AN EVIL PUPPET MASTER?!?
Mwa ha ha!
Hurry faster, or else it'll get cold!
TRUDGE!
Pre-emptive revenge is a dish best served lukewarm.
CHOMP
THEND

CHIPS and also SALSA
A Pirate Penguin Vs Ninja Chicken Cartoon Adventure
SCARMPF!
drip
NIMJAH JZHIKKIN!
Dude! Swallow!
I ain't gonna eat no salsa-less chippers! Why dint you doo the grossery shomping?
I've been busy, I'm trying to get caught up on all the singing cat videos before the new one comes out. Plus, snack shopping is YOUR chore.

STOB LOONKING AD STOOPID INNERNET THINGS AND DEAL WIF THIS ANGRY BIRD! RAWRGHSDKLXHG!
Woah! Are you choking?
KCHGX!
O My G! Don't die! I'll look up instructions for doing the Heimlich Maneuver!
GLEEP!
Umti-tum tum tum...
CHRT!
It says here I should... No... that can't be right...

Mm

HAIYAH!

Huf! Hof! Honf!
Ick.
HOF HOF
Thanks for heimliching me, buddy!
Ick.
And if we don't have any salsa, I'll just have to make some!
You want me to look up recipes?
Nope!
I'm a Culinary Mad Scientist! Let's see, Ketchup, Onions, Chiles, Tobasco, Eggs, Pizza Spice Packets, Curry, Strawberries...
CHUP
GLORMP!
AUGH!
...Tangy!
I got the whole thing! This is the best weird eating video you've ever accidentally made.
Oops, I filmed it tall-ways. Can you do it again?
Sure.
THEND

BREAKIN' STUFF
A Pirate Penguin Vs Ninja Chicken Cartoon Adventure
Hey Pirate Penguin, while you're doing laundry, would you wash my spare ninja pajamas?
NO! I don't want to!
WASH
JAM JAM JAM
TUESDAY
BLOOPa DOOP
SOAP
RUMBLE WUMBa WUUM
WEDNESDAY
Phew! There! All our Moonicorn Princess graphic novels are finally all arranged chronologically! Even the bootleg prequels, sequels, and in-between-quels!
Hmm...
SHOVE!
I wanted them arranged by color! RAWR! Rainbowetically!
CRANCH!

THURSDAY
Excellent pile of fried dinner things, Ninja Chicken!
Thanks! It's mostly old newspapers dipped in barb cue sauce. If you do the dishes, I'll get dessert.
BBQ
DISHES? I thought we were gonna get paper plates and bowls so I'd never have to do dishes again!
That's wasteful. Besides, what about the pots and pans?
Paper pots and pans?
And paper forks and spoons, I suppose?
NC! We'd get PLASTIC utensils. DUH!
Load up the dish-washer, NOW. I'll dip some newspapers in caramel.
You're using sugary deliciousness against me!
Yep!
Argle
Bargle
asser
assin
umble.
Hup!
THROW!

FRIDAY
JUMP!
CRANCH!
Pirate Penguin. Why you breaking so much stuff lately?
AM I? Heh heh.
Gee. We'll just have to go to the swedish furniture store!
Vikea? I hate that place now!
PLEASE oh PLEASE can we go back? They've got such great bargains!
You don't care about bargains.
And their Feud Court and their WONDERFUL WONDERFUL BATTLEDOME! PLEEEEEEEEEEEEASE can we go?
Well...
ViKËA

VIKEA ONLINE
VIKEA
You tricked me.
You make it easy.
INSTANT DELIVERY
Knock knock ding dong hoodily boo!
Hoodily boo?
PUF!
HOODILY! Boo!
Wizard Wombat! You work for Vikea now?
Yup! Instant Magical Delivery. Only 3 times more expensive!
IPS
ZING!
Sign here.
VIKEA

Hey! These instructions are written in weirdo! They're waaay too complicated!
WW! Can you just assemble these for us with your magical powers?
ZOM WOM WOM
...Nope. I don't do installation.
Bye!
PUF!
That guy is weird.
How do we even know him again?
I don't know...
THEND

What IS that wonderful smell?
Pop-corn.
Um... Is this a visual metaphor cuz the food smells so good? Or are you actually flying?
GRAVITUDE
A Pirate Penguin vs Ninja Chicken Cartoon Adventure
I'M FLYING! They say penguins can't, but I proved 'em wrong! I had a couple energy drinks earlier, and have been SUPER hyper! I'm actually flapping so hard it looks like my flippers are perfectly still!
Can I have a pomp-corns?
GLAAAR
Wait a minit! How can you even smell? You don't have a nose!
Mmm. Hmm?
Whenever you do smelly things, you say it's because you can't smell anything!
Penguins have secret tiny nostrils. I can only smell delicious things, like fresh cut grass clippings, popcorn pie, or yummy yummy raw fish guts.

So, you only see, smell, and hear the things you want to?
That is correct. Hey, do you hear any cookies baking?
Is that why you never seem to see any of the dirty dishes or vacuuming or laundry?
What? We don't have any of that stuff.
Do you wear contact lenses?
Yeah. HEY!
POIK
CUZ THIS THING IS FILTY!
GIMME THAT BACK! I need it for looking! You're not supposed to take them out! EVER!
You're supposed to take them out EVERY NIGHT.
Ohhhh...
Well, I do have an extra one. Let's give it a whirl.
WHOA

WHOOOOOOOA! Everything's in HD! What are all these... Things? I always saw everything as just blobs of color...
Those are the furnitures. Notice how the stuff on my side is nice and yours are broken.
Um, wait, what is happening? Why are you- oh right. That thing from before...
I can see outside time! Everything's purple! And Green!
We should probably get you some medical attention. How many energy drinks did you have?
SEVENTEENISH! I stayed awake long enough to binge all 486 episodes of Moonicorn Princess in their original swedish!
Freeeeeeedom!
Come back here!
Okay, we're gonna take you to see the Doctorologist. And then an EyeBallogist.
Maybe we'll be lucky and find somebody on your insurance who does both.
Pirate Insurance! Popcorn! Turn the rainbows back on!
You could probably also use a therapist.
And a dentist. I'm falling apart.
THEND

kicking and SCREECHING

A Pirate Penguin vs Ninja Chicken Cartoon Adventure

I don't WANNA!

Yes you DO!
DON'T!
Put your sweater on, it's chillly out!
AUGH! It's itchy and I hate it SO MUCH! You can't make me! You're not my Admiral Grandma!
Sheesh. Can your Admiral Grandma do THIS?
POKE! JAB! NERVE PINCH! PRESSURE POINT!
Nope. Her incapacitating nerve pinches were much more warm and snuggly.

PLOP!

I... I can't move!
Yeah, the Paralyzo Nerve-Pinch™ I gave you should wear off in a couple minutes. If your toes start feeling sneezy, don't blink or else you'll die.
Now, march your butt out to the car, mister!
Um, no? YOU'VE PARALYZED ME.
Oh, right. Hmm. I guess I didn't quite think that through...
Haha! I outwitted you! On accident...
Erg. Umf. You should lose some weight.
You should gain some strength!
Touché.
What a drag.
Ernk. Arnk! Umf.
BING!
Tadaa! I'll drive!
Hey!
NWJ

Pirate Penguin, you know you can't drive!
I can drive! I'm just not a very good driver! HUUUUGE difference.
Do you even have a driver's license?
I have a Pirate's License, it says I can do what I want.
Is that a real thing or a fake thing?
So's your face.
VROOOOOOOOM!
Where do you wanna go today? Only $12 per mile.
This is my car, so: No. Also, we're going to the museum.
Oh yeah, that's why I was complaining. I HATE mooseums! They're way too learningy!
We've been there before and you loved it.
Do I look like the sort of penguin that remembers the things I've done before? How many car chases can I get in?
None.
Only one? You're the worst passenger EVER!

So, howzabout instead, we drive somewhere really fun, like... Hawaii! Or Greenland!
I don't think it's possible to drive to either of those places.
Now, please drive us to the Unnatural Mystery Museum.
You think you're in charge and get to make decisions? That's so cute!
But yeah, I guess you're right, it's your car, we should go to the museum...
... IN GREENLAND! WOOOOO! There's no place greener or landier than Greenland!
Rawr!
Oop.
Astronaut Armadillo Sez:
Even I know it's stupid to wrestle in a moving car.
Woo WOo Woo!
GRR! ARG!
POLICE
ONE ARREST LATER:
Hmm! This is one of the nicest jail cells I've ever been in.

Okay: Prison! Ninja Chicken, wanna join the gang I just started?
We're in a holding cell. The other guy in here was arrested for too much spitting.
Exactly. You need protection. The initiation fee is 14 candy bards, and you have to get a tattoo of my face... on your face.
I'd rather join Spitty McGee's gang.
Okay guys, we'll let you out two ways. You can either pay us a buncha bail money, or you can do some community service, picking up trash at various places.
NC, get out your credit card and pay the man!
Um, we'll do the community service. Can we volunteer to clean at the Unnatural Mystery Museum?
NOo!
EpiLogue:
NC, this museum is awesome! They got dinosaurs and knights with swords and creepy mummies and biplanes! Why didn't we come here before?
Sigh.
THE END

Pirate Penguin vs EXISTENCE
PICK
PICK
PICK
Sigh. I wish I had a nose so I could pick it.
Mammals get all the fun, the lucky skunks.
Seventeen Hours Later...
Siiiiiiiiiiiigh!
You know Pirate Penguin, a watched pot never boils.
NINJA CHICKEN! I don't have time for your stupid kitchen wisdom!
I AM WAITING FOR THE MAIL TO GET HERE!

I picked up your mail this morning, it's on your desk.
What? How could you?!? I hate you sometimes.
You hate me... When I'm helpful?
Yes.
Fine, then cook your own dinner!
I didn't say I hated you THAT much. Just a lil bit.
Wait... Since when do I have a 'desk'?
4A
4Q
4B
4Z
You have a pile of pizza boxes I generously call a desk.
Yay! New magazine Thursday!
Buckineer Quarterly
Suave
WARNING: CONTAINS 40% GREASE
You'll read those, but not books? Ay yi yi.
Books don't have advertisments. Look! The new iPatch is out!
iPATCH
V. 2 has all kindsa new features, games, apps, snaps, and hapablaps! Mine is a V.1 All it has is Tetris and Qwiken.
You can play videogames with your eyepatch? Is that why you're always standing around with a vacant expression?
Uhhh...
THEND

FLEX
A Pirate Penguin vs Ninja Chicken Cartoon Adventure
Ernk
Arf.
ERK
oomph
Ploof.
Whatcha doooon?
Working out. Blasting my quads. Hoo ha!
Do penguins even have quads?
I dunno, but if I do, they're gonna be--
SO TOTALLY
BLASTED!
Ooh.
There. If I can lift this last weight, I will become SO BUFFTASTIC I will totally be able to beat up all of my enemies.
OH YEAH! I'm The Best Me I EVER WAS! In Your Face! My Me is better than Your You.
ERNK!

Ninja Chicken? Where'd you go? Why aren't you admiring my fantastic wonderfulness strength powers? Lifting weights with a hook is tricky you know.
Hmmm? Oh, sorry. I was using purely the strength of my feather fingers to cling to the ceiling. That's tricky too.
I think I can manage with just my toes though... Yoink! Gimme that weight, let's see me do some upside down reps. One! Two! Seventeen!
Hup Hup Ha!
Flippy Dippy! Downwards Groundwards!
Juggle!
Now, what were you saying about fantastic wonderfulness and strength powers?
Sigh. Listen. Stop juggling me for a second and i'll come up with a fantastic comeback.
THEND

Pirate Penguin vs The MOVIES
Hey Ninja Chicken- have you seen my banjo?
What? Oh yeah-- I accidentally smashed it into a thousand pieces and then set those pieces on fire...
I don't really like it when you play the--
I GET IT.
So what am I supposed to do all day?
Watch TV?
Oh right. I don't enjoy your trumpet playing either...
Wanna go to the movies?
With you? No.
Oh C'mon! It'll be dark!
Will you pay for my ticket?
No.
Are you SURE? I also have an ACCORDION!

MOONICORNS
THE KOOKIEST KOOKA-BURRA
THE LESSER OF TWO WEASELS
One adult and one whatever he is for the "Moonicorn Princess" gritty reboot please.
IN 3D! IN 3D!
You don't have enough eyeballs for 3D!
You're just jealous of my iPatch!
Sorry nerds, sold out. You should have camped last night like all the other weirdos.
NOOOOOOOOOOOOOOOOOOOOOOOOOOOOOOOOOOOOO
MOONICORN PRIME! WHY HAST THOU FORSAKEN ME?
There are still seats available for the 2:00 showing of "BucketHead Wilson."
NOOOOOOOO
Is it... a animated?
Nah, live action.
NO

Oh... My d- d- darling Lorretta!
Do, do you th... think you could ever... love a- a Buckethead like m...me?
Uh, probably not. Sorry.
BORING!
sigh.
Ahah! My harmonica will spice things up!
VFEET!
EXIT
OUT.
That's another place we're banned from. What is your problem?
I dunno. Want some free trash popcorn?
THEND

Pirate Penguin vs Ninja Chicken
Sport of Kings
Rock Scissors Papyrus
Scizzors!
Dragon! I win!
Awwwwww... I didn't want to lose...
THEND
Pirate Penguin vs Ninja Chicken
Ground Goodies
Ooh!
CRONCH CRONCH!
Ew! Gross! Don't eat stuff off the floor! What is wrong with you?
It's fine. I'm pretty sure it's a jellybean.
What if it had been dirt? or a bug?
Statistically, the things I eat off the floor are delicious!
THEND

NINJA CHICKEN VS THE BEAST
Ninja Chicken! NINJACHICKEN! NINCHAJIGGEN!
WAUK!
TRIP!
nhjachggn...!
FLOMP
WHAT TIME IS IT?
Uh... like, six-thirty?
I NEED THE EXACT TIME! Also today's date, year, and phase of the moon!
What are you, some kind of question machine?
No, I'm Pirate Penguin. For now...
FINE. It's Fleptober 47th, The Year of the Flying Squirrel, and the phase of the moon is "Awkward Teenager."
You're not a very good answering machine...
"Please leave a message after the beep. BEEEEP."
I just need to make sure it's not a full moon tonight, and I lost my calendar...

Are you trying to tell me that you are a werewolf?
NO. Wolves are mammals.
Birds have feathers y'see. I'm a weregoose... GURNK! The transformation's starting!
TRANSFOOORM!
Ha! You're funny looking.
HONK! HONK!
SNARL!
Wait, now you look kinda freaky.

Puh-lease. I have ninja powers, you know. I've dealt with hordes of demon-zombies before, a werewolf-penguin-thing is no match for the likes of me.
Glork!
Ho-hum. As everyone knows, you can only **kill** a lycanthrope with silver bullets, but you can certainly make them unconscious by cutting off their air supply.
Gassssssssszsp!
And now, some silver duct tape. Geddit?
That oughta hold him till morning.
TIME PASSES...
Oooonk.
Rise and shine, sleepy! I ate all your secret stashes of candy.

Oookay, unstick me veeery caaarefully.
YEEECH!
Uh, you lost a couple feathers there, buddy.
I gotta do a speed-molt and re-awesomize.
There is a secret place that I know of, where a wise woman will, with wisdom, heal my shattered soul.
Uh the haircut store is a secret?
Shh.
Fashion
Do you have an appointment?
Every month. My name is Pemberly Plunderman.
Is it?
Never give your real name at a beauty salon.
The more I get to know you, the more I wish I didn't.

Hiya HairCareBear! I needs some helps. Gimme the usual- only moreso.
I'll say! So, did I tell you about my nephew?
I didn't know you had a nephew...
I don't. I'm gonna pick one out from the store later.
BlahBlahBlahBlahBlah BlardyBlardyBlardyBlar WomphWomphWomf BlahBlahBlahBlahBlahBla WingleWangleWongle! Hahahahaha Blah BlahBlah BlahBlah BlahBlah BlahB
Uh huh.
SUAVE SWASH BUCKLER
Are you even listening to me?
NOPE!
Don't worry, he does the same thing to me.
SUAVE SWASH BUCK
Oh, you must be Ninja Chicken! Pemberly here talks about you all the time. Strange, I thought you'd be uglier.
Maybe you can convince your friend to buy this special medicated shampoo?
ANTI LYCANTHROPY SHAMPOO WASHES THE WEREWOLF OUT!
Now... Don't let him go outside without a jacket. Unless you want a penguinsicle...
Aw man! Can you cut it again, but leave it a little longer?
Don't shed in my car.
THEND

PPvsNC: SEAWEED SURPRIZE
G'm'r'n'n.
Pirate Penguin!?! I haven't seen you for days! I thought you moved out. Or died.
Yeah, I was just really tired, or sick or something, I forget. Now I'm super hungry. Are you cooking me breakfast? FOODIFY!
It's 5 pm. I'm making ME sushi rolls.
What's a sushi?
My favorite? It's kinda like a japanese burrito, only different.
You can make some too if you'd like.
I want a bacon sushi, with potato-chunkersTM, cheesy cheesersTM and EggBlaztrzTM.
Um, it doesn't really work that way...
I think my pickled ginger and sriracha would make you make this face...
BLEK!
Penguins would probably like sushi more if it had raw fish in it, y'know.
THEND

PPvsNC: THE SNACKTIME CONTINUUM
CHECKITOUT TROUT! I found a perfectly good Time Hat in the garbage!
Shh. Can't talk. Reading book.
Um... Ninja Chicken? That book is from, like, 1992. It's probably expired.
It's an old favorite of mine, I'm doing a re-read.
I have the DVD of the movie they made. Wanna watch it with me? I could use my hat to make popcorn EXTRA QUICK!
NO! Leemee alone!
DINOSAUR JONES Famous Author
1992
...and so, just when all hope seemed lost, Pirate Penguin appeared and punched the T-Rex in the face. "Rawr" it cried. And that's how I saved Fishmas. THE END.
typedy
typedy type
TIME•CHANGE
I don't remember any of that...

Ahhhhhhh. And now for no consequences whatsoever!
PAUSE RIGHT THERE!
The Society of Very Important Completely Original TimeTraveler Action Squad
Word!
The Space-Time-Continuum has enough to worry about without the likes of YOU messing it up further!
Astronaut Armadillo! You're a time traveler too?
I am in the future. Did you even see my future beard? It's pretty rad.
Time to nip this problem in the butt!
PÜF!
Dang. Now how am I gonna get home?
NOT IT!
NOT IT!
NOT IT!
Dang.
BONUS WISDOM: ASTRONAUT ARMADILLO SEZ:
Hey Kids! Never Cause Any Paradoxes. OR ELSE.
THEND

Ninja Chicken vs Communication

A Pilot Pangolin vs Not Ninja Squid Cartoon Nonventure

Umm nooooo...?
Didn't we return all those swords to their original owners?
FOLD
Nuh uh! In your bedroom, behind the decoy cupboard, in the fourth locked box underneath your ninja-school yearbook, there's a tube with the Cutlass of Infinitude and the Ectoplastic Scimitar. Can I please borrow one pleeeeeeeease?
You know an awful lot for someone who's never been to my apartment.
Oh, I've been to your place lots of times! Pretty much whenever you go out! Who do you think keeps overwatering all your plants?
Uh... uh... Kccccchhh! You're breaking up! Kccchhh! I'm going through a tunnel! Bye!
FLING
Looks like I'm not gonna get that sword, Uncle Krackey.
FOOLISH MORTAL.
I love you too.
So if we're allowed to just switch jobs and species whenever we want, maybe I should try being a Pilot Pangolin or something? I mean, I'm already perfect, but maybe I could be perfect in a completely different way?
I'm gonna go change our door locks, maybe buy new ferns, I don't trust these ones any more...
THEND

NINJA CHICKEN VS BOOKS
Wanna go get a refreshing smoothie?
OKAY!
JING
JING
JING
Waitaminit... this is a book store!
BEST SELLERS
WORST SELLERS
CELEB
SMOO
Book AND Smoothie store.
Also dvds and music and magazines and bicycles and umbrellas...
You tricked me! I HATE BOOKS!
SINCE WHEN? You liked it when we visited the library!
I don't remember EVER visiting a library.
CELEB
Really? The Librarian beat me up, you ate two books about ice cream? Nothing? Why is it that whenever you manage to change your opinion, or grow as a person, you then forget it all, regress and lose all your character development?
Oh, that. My brain is full of holes. Yup. I think it might be mice. Maybe termites.
SLURP
Hey, are we in a book store? I LOVE BOOKS!

Hey, what's going on over in that tiny corner?
It's a booksigning! Quick! Run away!
I BUCKET HEAD
Hello sir or madam! Please buy my book! I'm not allowed to go home untill I sell ten copies.
Uh... what's your book about?
About 150 pages. HAR! No, seriously, I wrote a biography of Elizabeth Heppinstall.
She wrote the famous 19th-century bromance novel "Bucket Head Wilson," you know.
I, BUCKET HEAD
Ooh, I loved that movie!
I HATED THE STUPID MOVIE! They changed the whole story!
BucketHead Farms grows celery, not rootabeggas! Plus everybody got married instead of dying!
How do you know?
I got an exclusive interview with Elizabeth's cousin's 3rd-grade teacher's mailman. He told me secrets.
What secrets?
BUY A COPY AND FIND OUT! HA HA!

How much to buy a copy of your book?
$149.95
Yeesh!
Yeah, the publisher isn't expecting to sell many copies, so they had to raise the price accordingly. It's basically economics.
Hey! All the pages are falling out!
Yeah, they do that. The publisher also used the cheapest glue possible, made out of slugs.
I BUCKET HEAD
By the way, you break it, you bought it.
But!
Too late! I already auto-graphed it!
I broke some things and have to buy them too. Here's the book I want, and the 87 I don't want are over there. Where's your credit card?
MOON KORNS
THE END

SEASONS BEATINGS: APPvsNC Holiday Adventure

Man, I have seven keyrings, and only three keys. What am I doing with my life?
H'lo.
WHAT ARE YOU DOING IN THERE?
4A
4Z
4Q
Mailcarrier Meerkat doesn't put up with my nonsense.
But you can't possibly fit inside that mailbox. You're huge.
HEY! I've lost weight lately! Haven't you seen all those "before & after" photos I've been mailing out?
EEEEEERNK!
It's no use. You're super duper stuck.
I'm super duper lots of things.
Hold on, I'll be right back.
Wait, don't go! I'm scared and lonely!
4Z

I mean... I'm tough and totally fine all by myself! Now cmon! Help a penguin out!
SPRAY GREASE
PSHHT!
*Cough*Hack* *Gorch!*
4A
4Z
4Q
CHUNKA WUNKA FRUNK!
SMEERP!
Tadaa! By the way, a letter arrived for you! I tried to open it but my shoulder was too dislocated.
Hey, nice keyrings!
SLIT!
Hey, Astronaut Armadillo invited us to a Barbecue! It's at his ranch!
Yay! Road trip! I'll go pack.
WHEEEEEE!
Can I come too?
4Z
4Q

NINJA CHICKEN
AND THE BBQ THAT COULD HAVE GONE BETTER
Is it ninety nine?
No.
is it seven thousand twelve hundred and six?
Nope.
Is it five?
You guessed that already.
CHIPS + CANDY
...Aaaaaand that's my eight-hour audio book, "The Joy of Folding Everything You Own Into Tiny Triangles" completed. What are you two doing?
We're playing Guess How Many Bottles of Beer Are On The Wall. I'm winning.
They're bottles of imaginary Root Beer, Ninja Chicken! I promise!
Ooookay. Well, my driving foot is getting tired. Does anybody else want a turn behind the wheel?
I only like driving off ramps through flaming hoops.
Ooh! Pick me!

Like, 12 Seconds Later
Wow, you'd think with extra arms I'd be extra good at steering, but no. Much much worse. Sorry!
If I was the captain of this car I'd throw you in the brig if this car were a boat.
Does anybody know how to fix... that?
I could change a flat tire if I had some molten rubber.
The tires are fine! It's the engine that's smashed!
Just trying to be helpful.
And what are YOU doing?
Hitchhiking.
One: there are no cars coming, and Two: You don't have enough thumbs.
I'm trying my best!
Why is nobody's best GOOD ENOUGH?
SHING!
Now THAT'S how you hitch your hikes!

Hi! We're trying to get to the Armadillo ranch. I think it's pretty close, do you know where that is from here?
Yup.
Hey- are you related to our friend Astronaut Armadillo?
Yup.
What's your name?
Argonaut Armadillo.
Can't leave this just lying around.
Good thing your car is made of plastic, Ninja Chicken.
Sooo...
Can I turn on the radio?
Nope.
What about me, can *I* turn on the radio?
Okay.
KcHHHH
I like it. It's got no beat, and a tune you can't dance to.
RANCH DILLO
WHAT'S THE DILLIO?
DIL 1

RANCHO DILLO
WHAT'S THE DILLIO
Howdy y'all! You made it! Took you long enough! Welcome to Rancho Dillo, home of ME, Astronaut Armadillo! Did you bring any big piles of meat for us to throw on the grill?
Grillify
PRO PANE
Um, were we supposed to?
Ninja Chicken, did you even read the fine print on your invitation? It's a BARBECUE. To not bring your host some meaty meats is the HEIGHT of RUDENESS!
Uh, I got an idea... Do you like seafood?
PIRATE PENGUIN! HOW DARE YOU!?!
Well, I suppose I could chop a few of my tasty tasty arms off for you guys, they'll probably grow back... That's a thing with squids, right?
What? NO! That's not what I meant. It's just... my hat is full of frozen shrimps.
Ew. Why?
Built in Air-Conditioning, plus a handy snack. Duh.

Let me introduce you to everybody! That's Auntie Tabithy!
Hello there!
That's Uncle Smokey.
Hewwo.
Uncle Argy you already know...
Yep.
And Gramma Wunkle-berry.
WHAT?
And this is a big pile of my cousins:
Lumpy, Bumpy, Numpy, Scrumpy, Jumpy, Wumpy and Jennifer.
HI!
Salutations!
Greetings!
Hola!
Are you a Ninja Rooster or a Ninja Hen?
You have a weird face.
SOMEONE'S BITING ME!
Whoa. There are waaay too many people, I can't remember all those names! I'll just call y'all Squampington to keep things clear.
Maybe we could wear nametags for you?
Sorry, Mrs. Auntie Squampington, I don't want to go around doing any reading either.

Oh, and these are the wasps we pay protection money to, to keep all the other insects away.
'sup.
These are the Corn on the Cobb Stabulators, but they're useless since SOMEONE forgot to plant any corns last season!
Sorry.
Now, let me show you the barbecue sauces. Very important stuff.
This is the Extra Chunky. This is Jale
This is Chipotle Mayonaise. This is F
This is Oregano Kaboom. This is El Dia
is El Diablo Muerte (Medium). This is pea
now how that got there. And this is Crazy Dav Loco
Tofu Soybecue SossTM wit Surprize.
Should I be taking notes?
Okay, everybody draw straws!
BBQ
Are we seeing who wins the cowboy hat?
NO.
Can I wear the cowboy hat anyway?
I guess.
Then I can wear your pirate hat! YARG! Ahoy Mateys! See? It all works out!
I drew the short straw.
That means you go first!
Are we playing a game? Horse Shoes? Hand Grenades?
No silly! You get to be the human target! We're gonna hunt you! With weapons!
blink blink
Come again?

Okay, you can wear my hat, but don't get any purpleyness or slime in it.
WHAT? What do you mean you're gonna hunt me?
It's a tradition at our family barbecues! Tracking and attacking someone cross country works up an appetite!
Don't worry, no one's died since, like, 2007.
Everybody grab a weapon and a satchel of paintballs! Then choose your vehicle!
Dibs on the helicopter!
I call the Motorcycle! Which one of you whippersnappers wants the sidecar?
Ooh! I want the horse! Hi Ho!
I think I'm freaking out a little bit.
You really should be using this time to get a head start.
SPLATCH!
Sorry. Finger slipped.
You are way too cool with all this.

Gotta get away from these MANIACS! I can't believe they're HUNTING ME! For sport!
At least if they catch me they won't eat me, everybody knows chickens don't taste good.
Yeeeeehaw!
Yaaahooo!
Yeehoo!
Yawhaw!
Tally Ho!
Portabello!
Dude, really?
What? I thought we were all just yelling silly stuff?
We were, yours was just the wrong kind.
Mine was pretty okay though, right?
Meh.
This is so stupid! I shouldn't have to put up with this, I'm a ninja for crying out loud!

Let's see, the Chicken's tracks go in this direction...
Wait! NO! They're tricking us. See? NC's running backwards. Oldest trick in the Ninja Book. Ninjas are the WORST.
OR! Maybe they're double tricking us, so we only think they're running backwards! You go that way, and we'll go this way!
Mmph!
What are you doing?
What are YOU doing? We're not helping these crazies! We're not on their team!
Well bless my tentacles, you're right! In trying to fit in with these armadillo ding-dongs, I totally lost sight of what's truly important!
Friends never hunt other friends for sport.
Nobody gets to pick on Ninja Chicken but me.
RING RING
Hi NC. Yeah. We got them heading in the wrong direction. What's the plan? Uh huh. Uh huh. AH! Yes! You're so good at plans.
Later...
Grandma! Refuel my chopper! This is the longest hunt we ever had! Apparently, Ninjas are very good at hiding! We've checked everywhere! Except...

BBQ Sauce Sneak Attack!
QQB
BBQ
Augh! The unhuntable become the huntees! That's never happened before!
En Garde!
Wait! Everyone! Stop fighting! The wasps are using this distraction to steal all the food!!!
Zing!
Heehee!
EDITORS NOTE: This is Wasps and Pasta Salad, which is not the same thing as Macaroni and Bees.

Heeheehee!
Hohohoo!
Everybody out of ammo yet? My eyes are getting spicy.
BLINK
BLINK
The most dangerous game sure builds up an appetite! No hard feelings, NC?
BBQ
No.
Hard feelings.
Who wants to have a dip in the lake to rinse off before the ants get us?
Go without me, I'm not big on swimming. I'll just use these paper towels.
DAB. DAB.
So that's it? We're just done and back to normal?
Sure!
I'll get the banjos, so we can have a hoedown.
Actually, you guys are really weird and I don't like it here. I wanna go home.
But Ninja Chicken! BANJOS!
I'm probably great at banjo cuz I have so many arms.
PLEERNK. ZWONK.
No.
But the car is still broken!
I'll give you a lift home. I'm sick of all my relatives by now anyway. Grandma! Load their luggage into my jet!

Can we keep the banjos? As a souvenir?
Let me see?
SNAP
No.
Someday I will get an annoying musical instrument you won't be able to destroy.
Here's some BBQ sauce for the road! The sky road!
Let's get together again real soon!
Bye! Most of you were nice, even if all of you were crazy!
Sorry I used all your paper towels.
Hee hee.
CRUNCH.
G'bye!
THE END

And Now! The Epic EPILOGUE

(The part of the story that comes after the actual story is over!)

On the long, awkward plane flight home, Astronaut Armadillo revealed that the reason he had invited everyone to a sinister barbecue trap was because his feelings had been hurt that one time. But then he couldn't remember what had happened that had upset him so much he felt the need to plan an elaborate revenge...

It was either because Ninja Chicken hadn't appreciated Astronaut Armadillo's lyrics when they all learned to play guitar together and formed a rock band, or maybe it had been that time Ninja Chicken invited him over for board game night and Pirate Penguin was the best at cheating, and didn't even give Astronaut Armadillo a chance to show off his cheating skills, #SELFISH.

Either way, they all had a good cry about it, Samurai Squid went on blubbering for a good forty-five minutes, but this was because they hadn't been invited to game night or guitar practice AT ALL, and so now they'd have to swear some squid revenge, which was seriously at odds with all their squid friendship.

Then a hole in the fabric of space-time opened up, and their plane flew into a QuantumMaelstrom™, and landed in the future. Everyone had to rescue their older selves from their evil robot duplicates. It took forever. Also, the robots weren't technically evil, but they were misinformed and very obnoxious. Some of them eventually saw the error of their ways. The battle was finally over when Astronaut Armadillo towed the moon to Earth and used its MoonPower™ to transform Pirate Penguin into the UltimateWereGoose™. Geese hate robots. Geese hate everyone.

Then Astronaut Armadillo founded the Society of Very Important Completely Original Time Travelers Action Squad, (whose other members are all robot-duplicates, obviously) and they created the time-hat to take everybody home, but first, they attended history's first dinosaur-rodeo. Pirate Penguin found a way to cheat at that as well. They all swore revenge.

THE END. But also, TO BE CONTINUED!

OUTRODUCTION BY RAY FRIESEN

Hello hello hello! Hello! Cartoonmonger Ray Friesen here! Welcome to the back of the book for the third collection of Pirate Penguin vs Ninja Chicken cartoon adventures! I could have welcomed you to the front of the book, but that's just not my style. I didn't invite you to read the secret forbidden collection of PPvsNC comics either, because those are so secret even I haven't read them! All I did was write the outroduction for it, and then drew everything blindfolded.

I'm getting off topic.

I'm here to answer all the burning questions about Pirate Penguin vs Ninja Chicken you've never had. ReadyGO!

What kind of penguin is Pirate Penguin?

Pirate Penguin is a Fairy Blue Penguin, from Australia. Yes, they're blue, and that's why Pirate Penguin is blue instead of black or green like other penguins. I still don't know why they wear a belt with no pants though. I am frequently forced to wear pants, and I hate having to wear a belt with them. Maybe I just drew Pirate Penguin slightly weird all those years ago, and now I'm stuck with it? I guess I used to draw them with a beard until I made them shave. Now they've never even had a beard at all! Any time you see Pirate Penguin with a beard, or their eyepatch on the wrong side, that's just a visual typo.

What's going on under Ninja Chicken's Ninja Costume?

They are a ninja. Their personal information and feather colors are a secret. Any inconsistencies are my fault. That's why their mask design doesn't make any sense. I am open to any and all head-cannons, because I too enjoy kabooming cannons out of my head. I'm weird that way. I'm weird lots of ways...

Who helps you color all your comics?

For the longest time, I was assisted by my pal and frequent collaborator Joe Heath (www.MintyPineapple.com) but lately they have a Real Job (whatever!) and so I have passed the coloring pencil over to young Jaden Marker (Boogtoons.com) who helped me complete this book, and doesn't make absolutely everything green and purple like Joe used to. They are both great humans. Possibly the best ever (although I haven't thoroughly checked).

By the way, the dialogue font I use was created by Missy Meyer, who deserves 27 appreciation units for her outstanding fontsmanship. Go use her fonts, they're awesome. (www.MissyMeyer.com)

If you have any additional questions, please consult future volumes in this book series (all 713 volumes, minus the secret forbidden collections, available next year. The next year from whenever you're reading this. Or maybe the year after.)

Goodbye!

Ninja Chicken Fanart by **Jaden Marker**

THE FINAL PIRATE PENGUIN VS NINJA CHICKEN STORY EVER*
*Not Really.
Oh, hullo NC. Didn't see you there.
Oh hey PP. What weird stuff are you up to today?
Well, as you know, I've been keeping excessive Battle Notes™ on all our epic fights, so I can finally figure out who's better, you or me.
Is it me?
Possibly. As you can see from this Excel spreadsheet--
That's a napkin.
-- I've won 487 fights, and you've won 487 fights, with 14 ½ ties.
How can you have half a tie?
There were a couple of our fights that you didn't show up for. I counted those as wins for me. There were also a couple that neither of us showed up for. I counted those as wins for me too.
MmHm. MmHm. That sounds a lil bit... cheaty?
NOD

So! If my mathulations are correct, we're about to have our ONE THOUSANDTH battle, which will decide once and for all WHO is the ultimate flightless fighter!
I thought the joy was in the journey, not the destination. The only losing move is to stop playing! Are you SURE you want to have a FINAL battle?
Winning is my DESTINY! I have to defeat our friendship ONCE AND FOR ALL!
Well then, couldn't we just flip a coin?
... Yeah, okay.
Fly brave and true, oh orb of randomosity.
FLIPPY!
FWOOM

I, uh, I never saw a coin catch on fire and explode before.
I thought for sure it was going to land on its edge, but that was way cooler.
Okay fine, go get all your favorite weapons and meet back here in 3 seconds.
ZOW!
YEEEEEEEE!
WOOOOOO!
27 action packed minutes later...
Sigh. Another tie. How does this keep happening? I'm so much more skilled and disciplined than you!
You could totally win in a fair fight, so that's why I make sure I never fight fair.
I gotta confess, I made up all those battle numbers. I have no idea how many fights we've been in.
I know. Wanna go get smoothies?
Nah... Too tired. Let's pay somebody else to bring 'em to us.
THE END

PiRATE PENGUIN VS NINJA CHICKEN
MACARONi &